For
Sol, Flora & Bobby

Millie and Bobby's favourite hobby was searching for sticks in the park.

Sticks were fun for prodding and poking...

and chewing and crunching their bark.

Tired from a morning racing around,
the friends settled down for a nap.

Under a tree they were snuggled and snoozing
when they were startled to hear a loud...

SNAP!

A CREAK came next
and then a CRASH!
And last of all a THUD!

"The greatest stick in the world!" cried Millie.
"It's landed in the mud!"

They pushed it and pulled it and rolled it along.
They were feeling rather proud.

When from behind a bush appeared a bear
whose groan was incredibly loud.

"There's something between my teeth," he growled.
"I tell you, it's unbearably sore.
Could I borrow some of that stick you have
to release the piece in my jaw?"

Millie and Bobby
regarded their prize
as clouds above
whirled and swirled.

If they gave the bear
a bit of their branch,
would it still be
the biggest in the world?

"Maybe not the biggest," Millie said,
"but Bear will be really relieved."
So they gave him a twig for a toothpick -
he gave them a hug, he was so pleased.

Millie and Bobby felt rather jolly
after helping the stranger in pain.
"And we still have the largest stick in the park
so we really can't complain!"

But not long later they met a squirrel who appeared to be distressed.

"I need to bury these nuts," he said,
"but at digging, I'm not the best."

The furry fellow looked at their stick
and made a heartfelt plea.
"A stick would push through this mud.
Could you spare a bit for me?"

Millie and Bobby, feeling sorry,
gave squirrel a length to keep.
"Oh, what a fantastic tool it is!"
And he smiled as he dug deep.

Child and dog and great big stick
continued their route by boat.
The frogs and fish all seemed fine
but the duck - well, it couldn't float!

"It's cramp," said Duck, "from all that bread!
It's given me indigestion!
I need something solid to hold on to.
Do you have a good suggestion?"

Bobby chewed off a chunk of branch
which Millie threw into the water.

Duck was saved and they headed to land
with a stick which was significantly shorter.

"Another stranger helped and happy.
I like how it feels to be kind!
Perhaps the rest should be kept for us
since it was OUR incredible find."

The clouds were grey and it had started to drizzle
when they came across the bunny.
It had long droopy ears and big brown eyes
and a nose which was terribly runny.

"My tent fell down and now I'm getting wet!"
Both Millie and Bobby frowned.
Since when did rabbits sleep in tents?
Weren't their houses underground?

"I'm claustrophobic," Bunny explained,
"I'm scared of going under.
Can I use that stick to fix my tent
before there's lightning and thunder?"

They looked at each other then at the stick,
And Bobby let out a loud yelp.
"It's no longer very big!" Millie said.
"But at least it can still be of help!"

"I can't thank you enough!" cried Bunny, as the storm began to roar.
"Now, come in, cuddle up! There's plenty of room on the floor!"

The stick had been so very heavy. It was good to have a break.
They snuggled up and told their stories 'til they could barely stay awake.

Later that night, asleep in their beds,
the stars above whirled and swirled.

What were the two friends dreaming of?

OF COURSE,

THE GREATEST STICK IN THE WORLD!

About the Author

Emily Benet is an author and illustrator.
She lives by the sea in Mallorca with her husband and two young daughters.
The Greatest Stick in the World features her brother's Boxer dog, who was rescued from a
rubbish (trash) bin and has become an online sensation.

You can read the book Bobby from the Bin (his origin story), watch his antics on social media
and see Emily's online sketchbook by scanning the QR

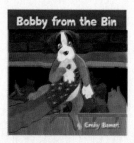

Please write a review

Authors love hearing from their readers!
Please let Emily Benet know what you thought about this book by leaving a short
review on Amazon or your other preferred online store.
It will really help other parents and children find the story!